The Amazing Adventures of

Chessie
the Manatee

By DAVID MESSICK

Illustrated by Liu Light

Dedicated to Frank Lakus
In honor of his many creations
for Rainbow Puppets

The Amazing Adventures of Chessie the Manatee
Original Chessie Puppets Created by Frank Lakus,
Laura Baldwin, Kathie Davis,
Christine Frank, and Helen Spaetzel
© 2021 / All Rights Reserved

Text and Puppet Photos David Messick

Illustrations: Lucia Liu

Page 32 images courtesy of Save the Manatee Club
SeaWorld Orlando activities conducted under permit #MA7701911
Page 33 Images by Rainbow Productions, Inc.
Page 34 and 35 images from Shutterstock

Designed by Lynn Mangosing

ISBN: 978-1-7332484-4-0
First printing / Printed in the USA

Rainbow Puppet Publications
18 Easthill Court,
Hampton, Virginia 23664

Rainbow Puppet Productions is a non-profit,
educational entertainment company

Thanks to
Traci Massie, Erin Matteson, Curtis Johnson and Optima Health
Chris Witherspoon, Lynn Clements, Beth Marshall
and the Virginia Aquarium and Marine Science Center
Luci Talbot Cochran, Erica Llera Mitchell, and Young Audiences of Virginia (Arts 4 Learning)
Norma Bigler and the Frog Prince Puppetry Arts Center and Theatre
Cora Berchem and Ally Greco of the Save the Manatee Club
Tony Gabriele, David & Stephanie Messick, Marcy Messick,
Marty Staton, Nancy Kent Swilley, and Rose West

Now Seemore doesn't miss a thing that happens on the bay.
So, when that seagull spotted something strange,
he stopped to say:

"Hey, Larry! Look! I think I see a giant swimming cow!
It started way out in the bay. It's getting closer now!"

His Loggerhead Sea turtle friend said, "That's no cow you see.
That creature comes from Florida, he's called a manatee."

"I started out in Florida, I swam and swam and swam.

Now could you kindly tell me just exactly where I am?"

"This bay is called the Chesapeake,
the biggest in the land.

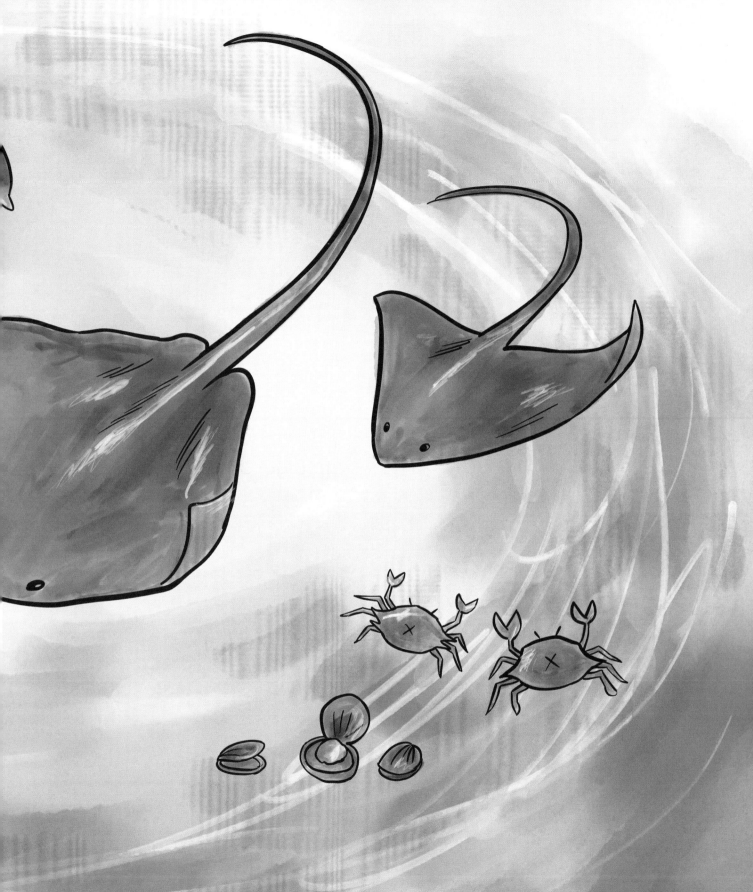

It's filled with dolphins, lookdown fish,
and sting rays, crabs, and clams!"

"You've gathered quite a crowd because you are a sight to see.

They've given you a nickname...
It's 'Chessie the Manatee!'"

Then Seemore added, "I would love to take you on a tour.
You've had a long, amazing trip. But, I can show you more!"

"Our blue crabs are a reason
Why the bay is so well-known.
Those hermit crabs use borrowed shells,
They cannot make their own.

That Fiddler Crab has one big claw,
As you can see him boast.
Our horseshoe crabs aren't really crabs,
Our ghost crabs aren't real ghosts!"

"Virginia is the perfect place to see a good horse race.
So now it's time to bet on which seahorse will win first place.

This daddy's watching his small fries, he cannot race today.
He carries them inside his pouch, then lets them out to play."

"Now, if you should get tired and you want to rest your head,
I really ought to warn you to avoid that oyster bed.

Some oysters like to make a pearl
while others like to sit.
But if you make them angry,
every one of them can spit!"

16

"But don't sleep now
because you'll miss a very lovely show...

See moon and stars way up above
and even down below.

Those graceful, gliding, glowing globes
are called moon jellyfish.

And look at all those Sea Stars.
Quick! It's time to make a wish!"

As Chessie chomps sea grass for breakfast, Seemore gives advice:
"That sandy grass will grind your teeth,
So, try these stale French fries."

But Chessie said, "No worries, I can eat five hours a day.
And I can grow some new teeth
When the old ones wear away."

This scientist is tracking where this dolphin may have been.
They recognize each dolphin by their pointy dorsal fin.

Those plastic bags and garbage can harm creatures in the bay.
These friends help out by picking up and taking trash away.

Then Chessie said, "Not everyone's a helper, I can see.
Some careless folks in motorboats hurt dolphins, fish, and me."

So Seemore said,
"We'll teach that fellow to respect the bay.
We'll ask that big Sand Tiger Shark
To help us save the day!"

Then, Chessie sneezed and said, "This tour around the bay was fun.
But now it's getting colder so I think I'd better run."

"Don't leave me now," said Seemore, "There are other sights to see.
You'll miss the eels and needlefish. And hey, won't you miss me?"

But Chessie said,
"I promise that we always will be friends.

28

I promise this is not how our amazing journey ends."

When Chessie said those words, I wonder how he could have known...
He'd swim to New York City and be featured in a show.

He visited a theme park and he flew inside a plane.
He even kept his promise to see all his friends again.

An Amazing Adventure!

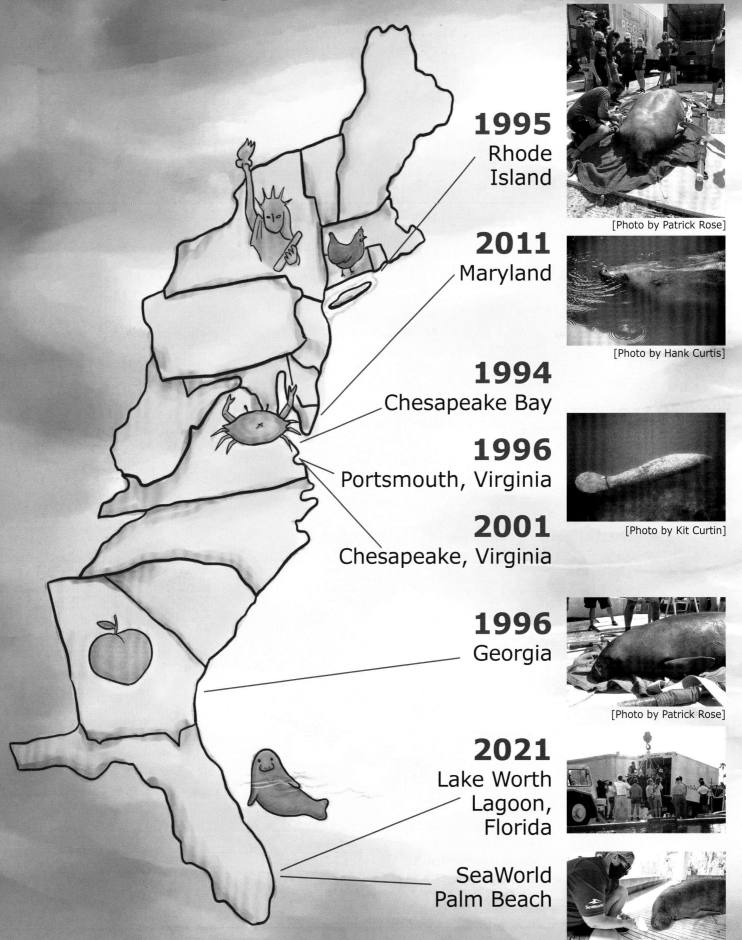

1995
Rhode Island

[Photo by Patrick Rose]

2011
Maryland

[Photo by Hank Curtis]

1994
Chesapeake Bay

1996
Portsmouth, Virginia

2001
Chesapeake, Virginia

[Photo by Kit Curtin]

1996
Georgia

[Photo by Patrick Rose]

2021
Lake Worth Lagoon, Florida

SeaWorld Palm Beach

[Courtesy SeaWorld Orlando]

A REAL Adventure!

Chessie's amazing real-life adventure began in 1994 when the manatee travelled from Florida to the Chesapeake Bay. Chessie became a star, drawing news-crews at every sighting. When Chessie didn't immediately return home as the weather got cold, he was given an airplane ride back to Florida.

Chessie returned to the Chesapeake Bay in 1995 and then headed past New York all the way to Rhode Island. This time, he swam back to Florida on his own.

In 1997, Chessie's adventure to the Chesapeake Bay was turned into Rainbow Puppet Productions' most popular musical. Life sized puppets shared the story of Chessie and other animals found in the bay.

The show was produced in collaboration with the Virginia Aquarium, the Chesapeake Bay Restoration Fund, and Young Audiences of Virginia. Hundreds of performances included sold-out stops at the Grand Opera House and the Smithsonian Museum of Natural History. An audio edition of the story was narrated by Broadway Superstar Carol Channing who also recorded a new song as a glamorous octopus in the waters of New York.

In real life, Chessie continued to make rare appearances in 2001, 2011, and 2021. During that last sighting, he was in need of medical attention and received it from staff at SeaWorld Orlando.

Organizations like the Save the Manatee Club work to provide protection and awareness of Chessie and his fellow manatees.

Josh with Chessie.

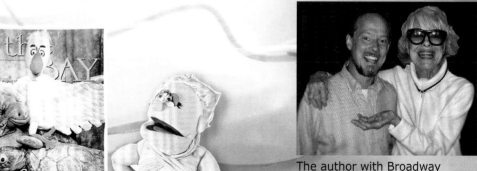

The musical was presented at the Smithsonian Natural History Museum. Here is the cast with Senator Patrick Leahy.

Long ago, some people would mistake manatees for living mermaids. We don't think they look alike. Do you?

The author with Broadway legend Carol Channing. She narrates the audio version of this story.

Amazing Creatures!

Manatees are large marine mammals. They breathe through their nostrils and usually come up for air every ten minutes. They do have tiny ears behind their eyes. They grow to up to ten feet and can weigh 1,000 pounds. Manatees eat for over five hours a day. When their teeth wear out, they can grow another pair. Manatees are threatened by motor boats and most adult manatees have many scars to prove it.

Loggerhead Sea turtles were once mistaken for floating logs. That is how they got their name. The markings on their heads are unique, almost like a fingerprint to a human. This is how you can tell one sea turtle from another. Plastic shopping bags look like jelly fish when in the water. They pose a danger if eaten by Sea turtles.

Horseshoe Crabs are not really crabs. They are more closely related to spiders. They are considered "living fossils" because they have stayed almost unchanged for over 450 million years. Horseshoe crabs have nine eyes located across their bodies.

A seahorse baby is called a "fry." It is the dads that take care of the babies after they are born. The fathers carry them in a pouch, much like a kangaroo. Seahorses have a prehensile tail, like a spider monkey. The tail is a like a hand they use to hold on tightly to sea grass.

Gills or Lungs or What?

These shiny, flat fish that seem to be looking at the ground are called Lookdowns. Their eyes are high up on their heads and their mouths are down low. These fish are found from Canada to South America and are plentiful in the Chesapeake Bay. Behind their eyes you can see slits which are called gills. The gills allow the fish to breath underwater. They don't have to come to the surface to catch a breath like people do.

Dolphins do not have gills, so they are not fish. They are marine mammals. They have a blow hole on the top of their heads and must come to the water's surface to get air. Marine scientists can tell one dolphin from another by the shape of their dorsal fins.

Sand Tiger Sharks have gills to breathe underwater. Yes! Sharks are fish. The Sand Tiger has two same-sized dorsal fins which makes it easy to recognize. While they have a scary double-row of teeth, they usually stay on the ocean floor and are not a danger to humans.

Sea Stars don't have gills and they don't have a blow hole. They are not fish and they are not marine mammals. What Sea Stars do have are hundreds of tiny suction cup feet. They get oxygen from water moving through their skin and feet.

Since they are not really fish, it's best to call them Sea Stars, not Star Fish.

David Messick is the founder of Rainbow Puppet Productions. He has written several children's books and dozens of original children's musicals that have been performed at the Smithsonian, New York's American Museum of Natural History, and many other organizations. He has also worked on development projects for the Oprah Winfrey Show and the Disney Channel and worked with many legendary performers. He and his wife Marcy are the parents of two amazing young men… Joshua and Luke.

http://davidmessick.com

Liu Light is an illustrator and multimedia designer in New York City. Light has illustrated a number of children's books with a focus on books featuring diverse voices and stories for such organizations as Shout Mouse Press and Rainbow Puppet Productions. They also enjoy drawing animations and comics.

http://liulight.com

Other books from David and Liu:
Never Give Up, Short Stories about Big Dreams
Creatures Great and Small
Mary Peake and the Mighty Acorn
Open a Book
The Tall, the Tough, and the Tiny

Audio Programs by David Messick
And the Rainbow Puppets
"The Amazing Adventures of Chessie the Manatee"
"From the Sea to the Sky"
"Jonah"
"The Mother Goose Travelling Rock and Roll Show"
"A Pirate Party"
"The Really Big Dinosaur Show"
"Toyland!"
"The Wetland Revue"
"The Wright Brothers— See Us Fly!"

Available at
Amazon.com, RainbowPuppets.com,
and DavidMessick.com